A Bed for Kitty

Yasmine Surovec

ROARING BROOK PRESS
New York

Kitty loves sleeping.

And Chloe loves Kitty.

Kitty is curious.

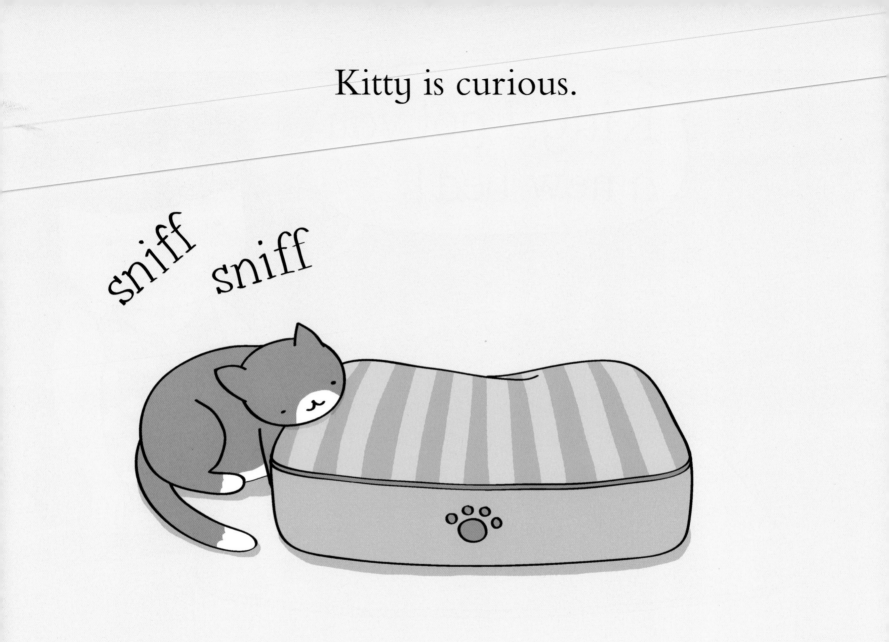

sniff sniff

scratch

scratch

roll

roll

But Kitty does not love her new bed.

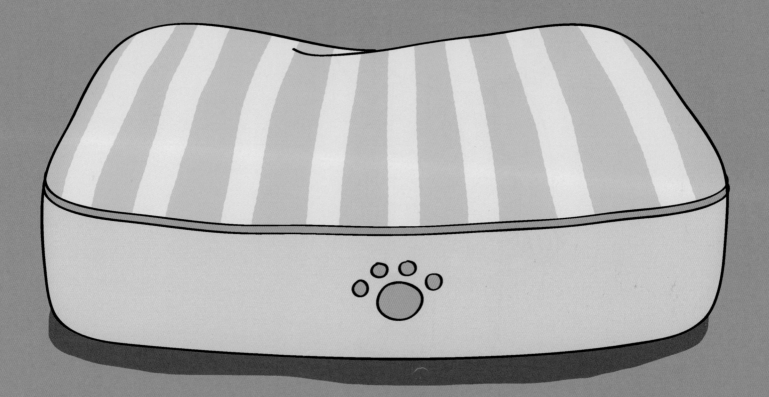

Kitty sleeps on Chloe's chair,

and in her litter box!

But Kitty does not sleep on her new bed.

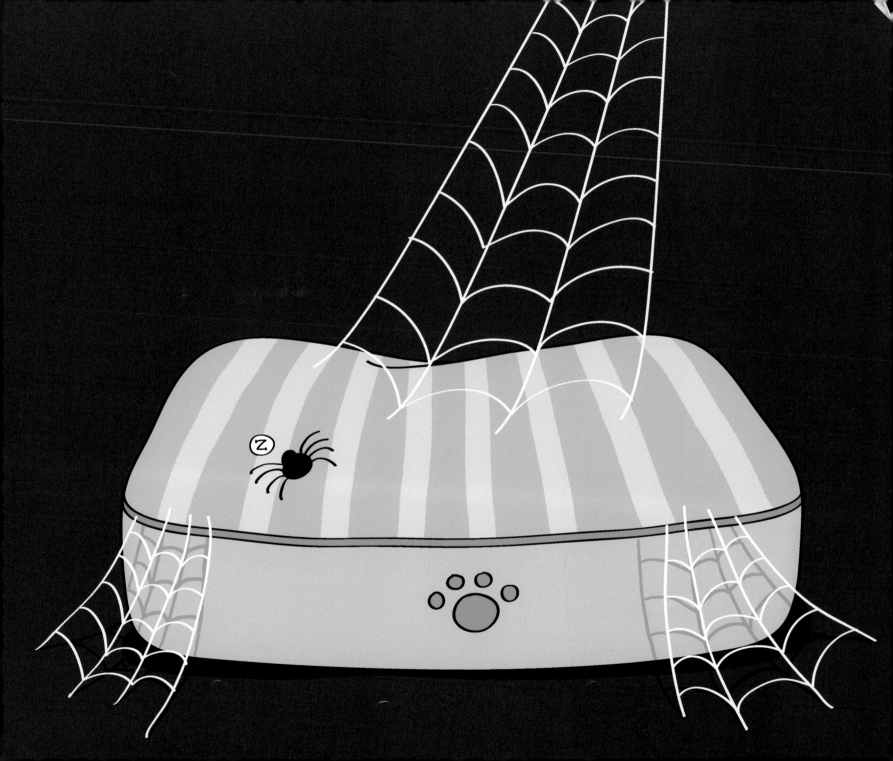

Kitty sleeps on Mom's favorite sweater,

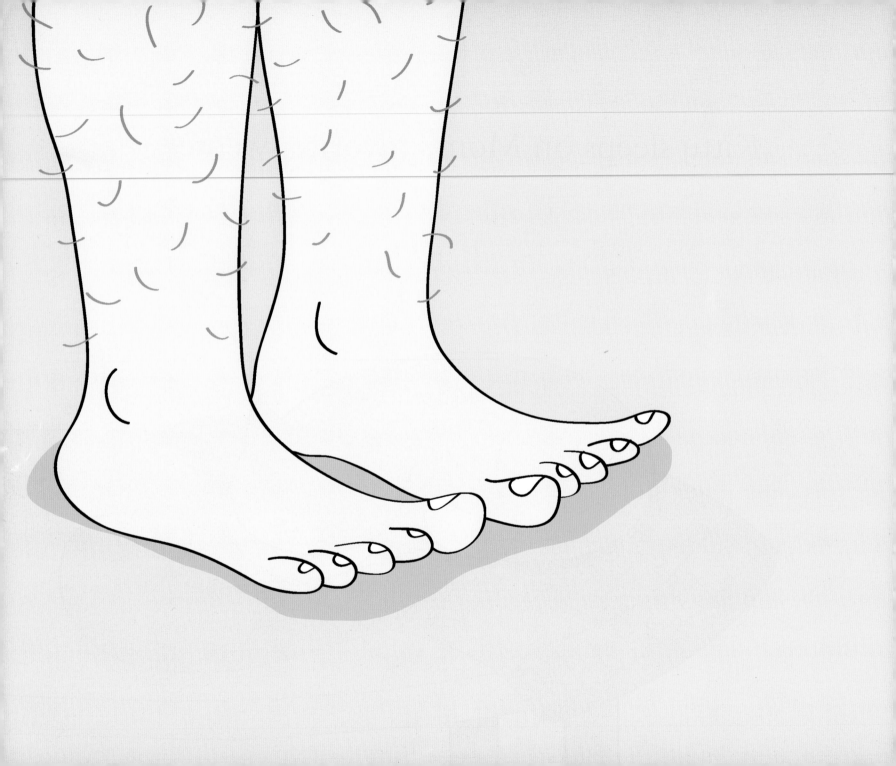

and on Dad's old slippers,

and in Chloe's sock drawer,

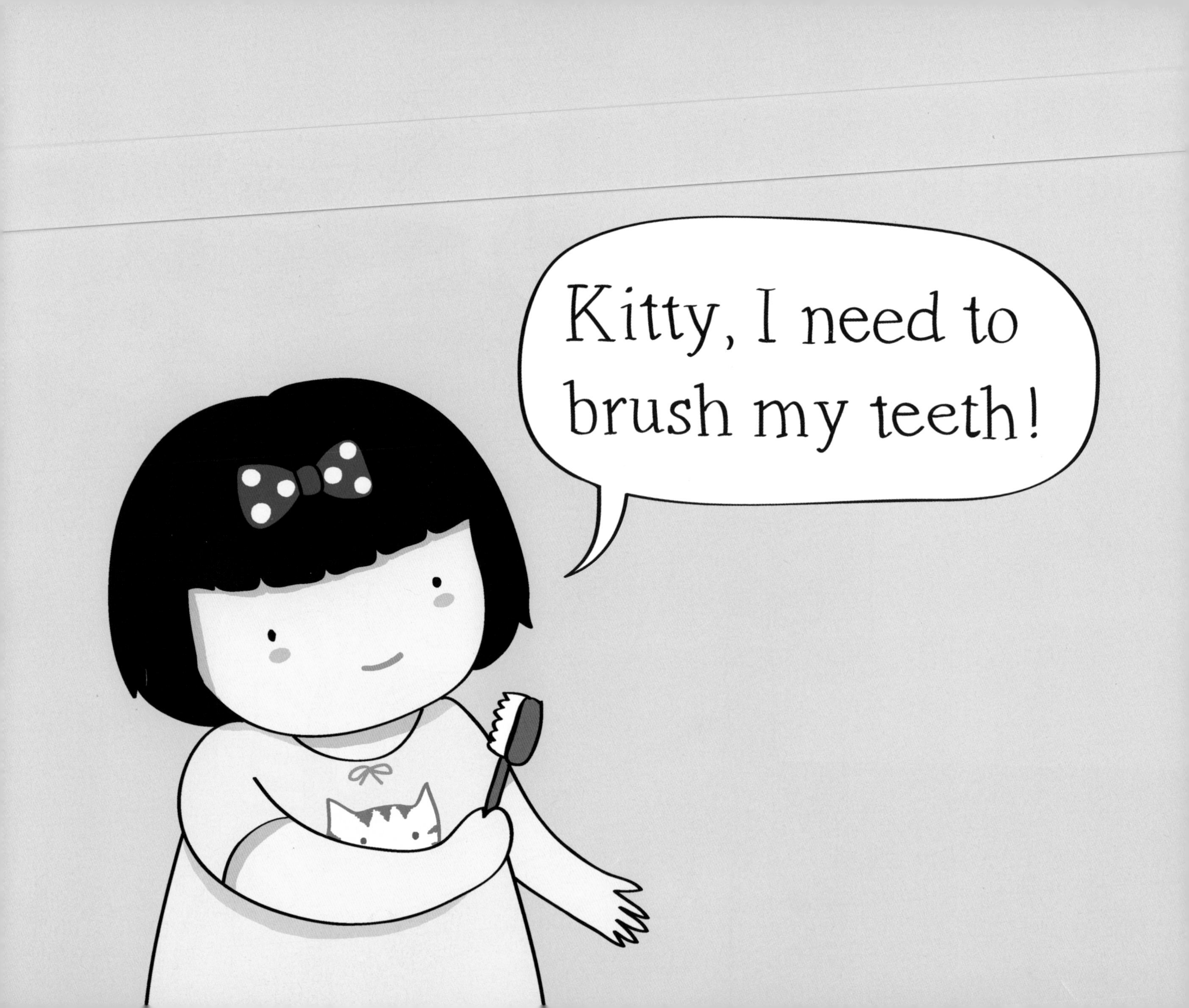
Kitty, I need to brush my teeth!

and in the sink!

But Kitty does not sleep on her own bed.

Goodnight, Kitty.

Library of Congress Cataloging-in-Publication Data
Surovec, Yasmine, author, illustrator.
A Bed for Kitty / Yasmine Surovec.— First edition.
    pages cm
    Summary: Kitty sleeps in unlikely places all around the house—
but never in her own bed—until Chloe discovers the perfect sleeping
arrangement.
    ISBN 978-1-59643-863-7 (hardcover)
    [1. Cats—Fiction. 2. Sleep—Fiction.] I. Title.
PZ7.S965626Be 2014
[E]—dc23

NOV 0 3 2014

                                                            2013033515

Roaring Brook Press books may be purchased for business or promotional use.
For information on bulk purchases please contact Macmillan Corporate and Premium Sales Department
at (800) 221-7945 x5442 or by email at specialmarkets@macmillan.com.

First edition 2014

Book design by Roberta Pressel
Printed in China by South China Printing Co., Ltd. Dongguan City, Guangdong Province

1   3   5   7   9   10   8   6   4   2

also by Kathy Hoopmann

All Cats Have Asperger Syndrome
ISBN 978 1 84310 481 0

Haze
ISBN 978 1 84310 072 0

Asperger Adventures

Blue Bottle Mystery
An Asperger Adventure
ISBN 978 1 85302 978 3

Of Mice and Aliens
An Asperger Adventure
ISBN 978 1 84310 007 2

Lisa and the Lacemaker
An Asperger Adventure
ISBN 978 1 84310 071 3

KATHY HOOPMANN

all dogs have ADHD

Jessica Kingsley Publishers
London and Philadelphia

First published in 2009

by Jessica Kingsley Publishers
116 Pentonville Road
London N1 9JB, UK

and

400 Market Street, Suite 400
Philadelphia, PA 19106, USA

www.jkp.com

A CIP catalog record for this book is available from the Library of Congress
Hoopmann, Kathy, 1963-
  All dogs have ADHD / Kathy Hoopmann.
    p. cm.
  ISBN 978-1-84310-651-7 (hb : alk. paper)
  1. Attention-deficit hyperactivity disorder--Juvenile literature. 2. Dogs--Behavior--Juvenile literature. I. Title.
  RJ506.H9H663 2009
  362.196'8589--dc22
                          2008017777

A CIP catalogue record for this book is available from the British Library
British Library Cataloguing in Publication Data

ISBN 978 1 84310 651 7

Printed and bound in India by
Replika Press Pvt Ltd

To Janet Eiby,
who understands

Introduction

Children on the Attention Deficit Hyperactivity Disorder (ADHD) spectrum can have problems in three main areas.

- They may find it hard to keep focused.
- They may be hyperactive.
- They may be impulsive.

Of course, everyone finds it hard to focus, or they are hyperactive or impulsive occasionally. The term ADHD is only used when a person has these traits so often that it disrupts their lives.

But as you read, remember that not every child with ADHD has all the traits mentioned in this book. There are ADHD kids who are very active, and those who are not. Some may be outgoing, and others very shy. But all children with ADHD need understanding and love. They need specialist help which may include medication and behaviour management.

Most of all, children with ADHD need people who believe in them, people to build their self-esteem, and people to go on life's journey with them, wherever it may lead.

Attention Deficit Hyperactivity Disorder
may be detected soon after a child is born.

**An ADHD child may not sleep
          as much as his parents would like.**

His first steps aren't steps...

**they are an attempt
to escape,**

because the world
        was meant to be explored.

He knows what he wants
and he wants it NOW.

When opportunity

presents itself,

he goes for it,

and may dive straight into a situation

without thinking of the consequences.

An ADHD child can be fearless,

but
unfortunately,
his body is not
so invincible.

He is easily
disorientated,

he's always losing things,

and often
can't find
what is right
in front of
his nose.

When playing, he may not be sure
how to take turns, or how to share,

and he can be
rougher than
he intends.

Others may not invite him to join their games,

which is sad,
because he
has a loving,
caring nature,

**and he can be
so much fun!**

An ADHD child can be distracted by things other people don't notice,

and his
priorities may
differ from
those around
him.

"But this is
important."

His mind works better
    when his body is in motion
        and he finds it hard to sit still for long.

His senses can go into overload
with everything going on,

so he goes from one task
to the next without
finishing anything.

Books can be hard to understand,

and things learnt are tricky to remember.

"Oops, that's right, cats don't like hugs!"

He doesn't know where to start,

"This way, no, that way!"

and even if there are instructions, he may not know how to follow them.

"So what do I do after I touch my toes?"

There's no doubt he is very bright,

"I was just checking if the sprinkler worked!"

but not everyone
appreciates his type of intelligence.

So although
he tries hard
to be good,

those in charge
are not always
impressed
with his behaviour,

and he is often labeled a clown.

He is easily bored, and when that happens,
his mind fogs and his eyes close all by themselves.

'Somewhere
else' can seem
so much more
interesting,

and he dreams of escaping things that don't interest him.

Time can pass
without him noticing,

and he can end up in the doghouse

without knowing why.

People keep saying
"You can do better if you try harder,"
but it's simply not true.

Life is so darn frustrating!

When things
get too much,
he may
tantrum.

Being very sensitive, he gets sad

because he wants to be like everyone else,

but he just can't.

Those who love him become sad too,
because they don't understand
why he behaves the way he does.

Sometimes others think
they can bring him up better
than his parents can.

But when he finds something he likes,
       his concentration is fierce,

and his
dedication
to the task
is whole
hearted.

His mind is often
    miles ahead of his peers,

he sees the 'big picture' easily,

and he can find solutions
    where others don't think to look.

His creativity is legendary!

As an ADHD child grows older,
he can do anything he wants,

**and he is always willing
to try new things.**

When life seems the same, day after day,

he knows it's time for a change.

But when he finds a job he loves,
    his amazing sense of intuition,

his drive to
achieve in
his interest
area,

**and his
bubbly
nature,**

means he
can reach
the very top
of his
chosen field,

like many with ADHD before him.

"Henry Ford"

"Leonardo da Vinci"

"Alexander Graham Bell"

Sure, he may not worry
    about his looks, and he has
        his own way of doing things,

which is fine,
      because if everyone was the same,
            life would be very boring indeed.

So when an
**ADHD child
has love and
support,**

good friends who accept him just the way he is,

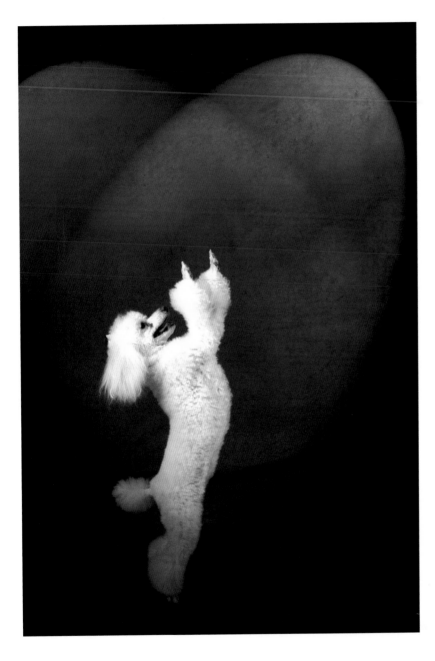

**encouragement
to pursue his
dreams,**

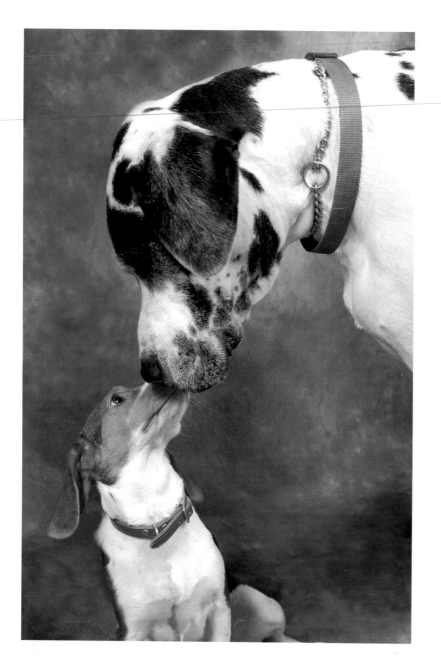

**and someone
to believe
in him,**

JUN – X 2011